# OLIVIA™
## and Her Ducklings

D0169791

adapted by Veera Hiranandani
based on the screenplay written by Eryk Casemiro and Kate Boutiler
illustrated by Shane L. Johnson

Ready-to-Read

Simon Spotlight
New York   London   Toronto   Sydney

Based on the TV series *OLIVIA*™ as seen on Nickelodeon®

SIMON SPOTLIGHT
An imprint of Simon & Schuster Children's Publishing Division
1230 Avenue of the Americas, New York, New York 10020
For information about special discounts for bulk purchases, please contact Simon & Schuster
Special Sales at 1-866-506-1949 or business@simonandschuster.com.
Manufactured in the United States of America  1210 LAK
9  10
Library of Congress Cataloging-in-Publication Data
Hiranandani, Veera. Olivia and her ducklings / adapted by Veera Hiranandani ;
based on a teleplay by Eryk Casemiro and Kate Boutiler. — 1st ed. p. cm. — (Ready-to-read)
"Based on the TV series, Olivia as seen on Nickelodeon"—C.p. ISBN 978-1-4169-9079-6
I. Casemiro, Eryk. II. Boutiler, Kate. III. Olivia (Television program) IV. Title.
PZ7.H597732501 2010  [E]—dc22  2009007381

is painting a picture of .

OLIVIA                                                                                                    IAN

But  will not stand still.

IAN

He has an itchy nose.

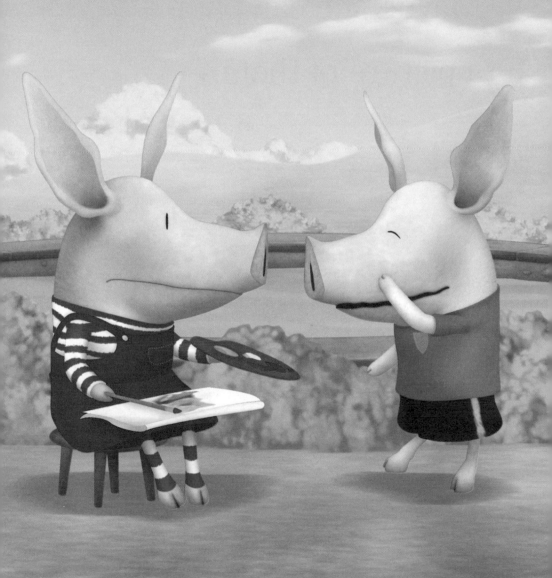

OLIVIA looks for something else

to paint.

She sees some  DUCKS .

Maybe she can paint

a picture of them.

"Poor little  DUCKS ," says OLIVIA .

"They want their mother."

The  **DUCKS** cannot climb the  **HILL**.

**OLIVIA** and **IAN** help them.

"Come on, !" says .
DUCKS          OLIVIA
"Quack!" says  .
IAN

They did it!
OLIVIA
wants to stay with
the .
DUCKS
But it is time to go home.
"Good-bye, !" says .
DUCKS
OLIVIA

At home,  paints
OLIVIA
a picture of  .
FLOWERS
She paints her
FLOWERS
 ,  , and  .
RED      YELLOW            PINK

Quack!

"Very funny, . Please stop,"
says  .
"Stop what?" asks  .

"Look!" says  .

OLIVIA

"The  followed us home!"

DUCKS

"I guess they really, really like me!"  OLIVIA says.

"Quack!" say the DUCKS.

's mom sees the .

OLIVIA · · · · · · · · · · · · · · · · · · · · · · · · · DUCKS

"Can we keep them?"

asks .

OLIVIA

"I'm sorry, .

OLIVIA

The ⬭ is their home,"

POND

says her mom.

"The  have to
go back in the morning,"
her mom says.

DUCKS

At least the  can stay for a little while.

"Who wants to play hide-and-seek?" asks.

"I do!" says .

"Don't look behind the !"

 shuts her eyes.

She counts to three.

looks in the kitchen.

OLIVIA

She does not see any  .

DUCKS

**OLIVIA** looks in the living room.

But she does not see any  **DUCKS** .

 cannot find the .

"! Please help me!" calls .

" ! I know where
OLIVIA

the  are!
DUCKS

Come to the bathroom!"

says .
IAN

The  are in the bathtub!
DUCKS

"Just because I hate baths

doesn't mean DUCKS

hate them too," says IAN .

After their swim,

it is time for bed.

"Would you like me to read

you a  ?"

BOOK

 asks the  .

OLIVIA                    DUCKS

But the  are asleep.
DUCKS

"Good night, ," says .
DUCKS                          OLIVIA

Soon  will be asleep too.
OLIVIA